The Saving of Sly Manatee

To the CHILDREN of
SIOUX CENTER,

LOVE NATURE!
ENJOY READING!
CARE FOR YOUR
ENVIRONMENT!

[signature]
3·29·2000

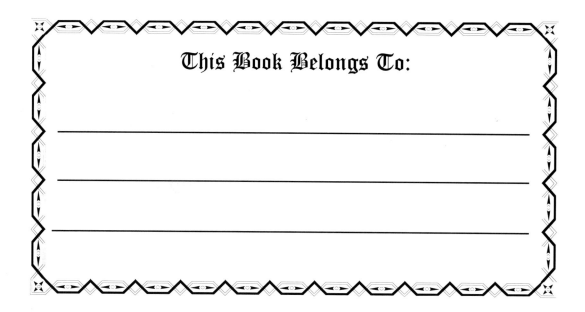

This Book Belongs To:

_____

_____

_____

The Saving of
Sly Manatee

by John Harms II

Illustrated by Robin Lee Makowski

Edited by Robert Franklin Spencer

Frederick Press ~ Palm Beach Gardens, Florida

Library of Congress Catalog Card Number 98-93224

ISBN 0-9653871-3-5

Printed in the United States of America

Dedicated to my brother, Hank

for the good times we shared exploring, and for our love of the sea.

Company Philosophy

Frederick Press strives to inspire children to realize the importance of caring for their local environment with a positive active role. By showcasing interesting animals that are common to areas, children learn to relate to the needs of their own surroundings. Frederick Press hopes children will become more aware of their natural environment, by enjoying the adventures of a boy named Buster and the animals he encounters.

When people take proper care of their local ecology and are responsible when visiting other areas, the earth's environment will improve and be a better place for all living things.

Frederick Press donates a portion of its revenue to benefit the rehabilitation of injured and orphaned animals, support zoological parks, and save manatees.

TABLE OF CONTENTS

*Glossary words are *italicized* throughout the story for easy reference.

CHAPTER 1

~Manatees on the Move~

Whoosh! The baby manatee zoomed around his mother, looking for something to do. They were staying at the *warm water discharge* of the power plant, and his curiosity was getting the better of him. After chasing a barracuda that shared the area, he swam into the cool water beyond the discharge area. It wasn't long before his mother gently directed him back.

His three-year old sister swam up to them and let out a string of whistles and squeaks. She had just returned from *foraging* among grasses and plants in the lake. The water was getting warm enough to move to their spring feeding grounds.

The mother nudged her baby and led him and his sister into the lake.

"Finally, something to do!" The baby thought as he swam next to his sister. They swam south of the discharge area into the murky water of the lake. This was the first time he had experienced the open water with boats buzzing by him.

A boat came straight at them. Just in time, his sister took a deep breath and dove, or *sounded*, making a large splash with her tail. He copied her and hugged the bottom. He felt the water push him as the propeller just missed them. The adventuresome calf, no longer feeling brave, swam very close to his mother for the rest of the trip.

His mother's back had visible prop scars from similar encounters with boats.

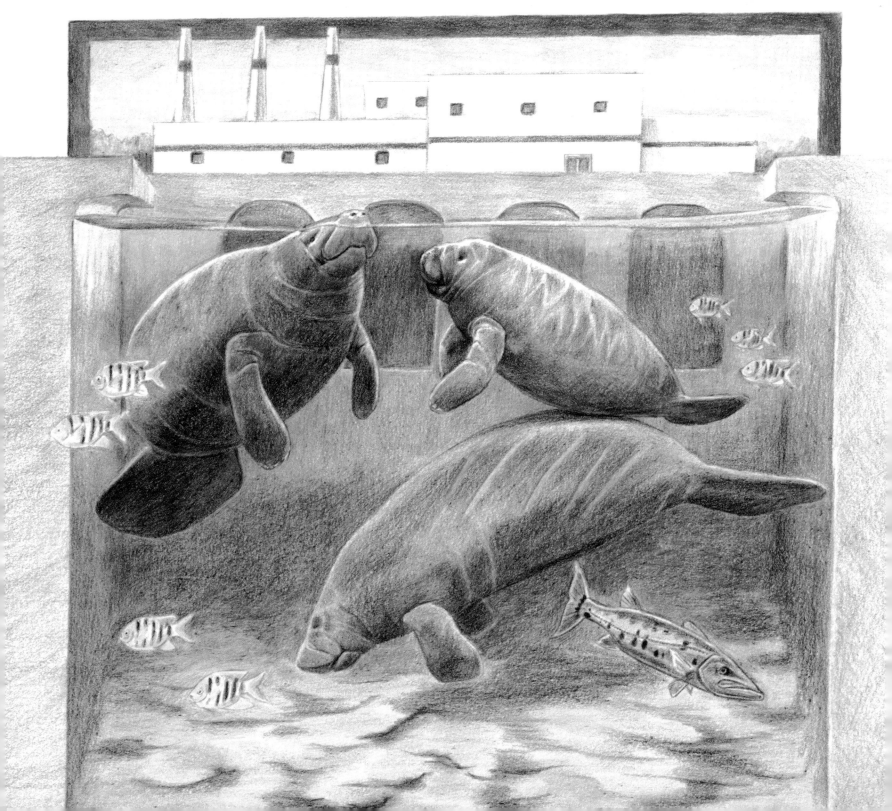

After about two hours of swimming, his mother turned into one of the canals off the lake. As they swam past a spoil island near tangles of *mangroves*, he felt his curiosity returning. His mother stopped in an enlarged part of the canal and allowed him to explore. Mullet were swimming in and out of the *mangrove* roots as the calf rolled upside down to get a closer look.

When he returned to his mother, she was chewing on something he had never seen before. It was a strange green plant that floated in the water. Its roots dangled beneath the water with shrimp swimming in and out. The stems bulged out and turned into a flat leaf with colorful flowers on top. His mother pushed some over to him. He bit down on the bulging green part.

"Poof!" The plant popped.

"What a terrific taste!" The calf thought as he munched on the delicious water hyacinth. This new taste became his favorite.

He gobbled down another and another, until he couldn't eat one more bite. There were hyacinths everywhere.

"Wow! There are so many places to explore and hyacinths to eat. I'm going to stay here forever," he assured himself as he nuzzled his mother.

CHAPTER 2

~A Friendship Begins~

"Dad! Dad!" Buster said as he ran into the house from his practice with his swim team. "He's back! He's Back!"

"Dad's not home from work yet. Who's back?" his mother asked as they hugged.

"Valiant, Mom. The bird we rescued. He's back. Rob Fisher said he saw a great blue heron with a leg band just like Valiant's," Buster explained.

"Where did he see him?" she asked.

"In the *mangroves* by the canal. He thinks he might be building a nest," Buster said excitedly.

"Take your old spotter's scope and find out if it is Valiant," his mom said handing him the telescope.

"Thanks Mom," Buster said as he ran to his room, grabbed his backpack, zoomed out the door and jumped on his bike. Riding fast, he saw Rob in his front yard.

"Rob, come on! Let's go see if it's really Valiant."

"Race you there!" Rob yelled, as he jumped on his bike.

They raced down the tree lined path, to the dirt road that led to an abandoned marina. The canal served as a route from Lake Okeechobee to West Palm Beach in the early 1900s. A *lock* and *spillway* separated freshwater from saltwater to protect the inland environment.

Getting off their bikes, they ran to the stairs. The weather-beaten dock shook as they carefully walked to the end near the heron. Manatees were feeding between the docks.

"Hey, look!" Rob said. "There's a baby manatee with its mother."

Just then, a heron flew over their heads and settled in a *mangrove* tree about fifty feet from where they stood.

"Did he have the band on him?" Buster asked, grabbing his telescope.

"I don't know," Rob said, turning around. "I just saw him land."

Sitting on the dock, Buster studied the heron with his scope while dangling his feet in the water. The baby manatee had seen humans before, and swam closer to get a better look at Buster's wiggling toes.

"It could be Valiant," Buster whispered, not noticing the baby manatee.

Hovering around Buster's toes, the calf thought to himself, "I'll grab one and see what happens." With that the calf reached up, slurped Buster's big toe and pulled it under.

"Whoa!" Buster yelled, losing his balance.

Splash!

Rob had just enough time to grab the scope from Buster's hands and toss it on the dock. He was laughing so hard he lost his footing and fell in next to Buster.

Splash!

The manatee brushed Buster's back as it swam under him. Its coarse skin reminded him of the elephant he once rode at the fair.

"Did you see that?" Buster asked.

"Yeah, it was the baby manatee," Rob said laughing. "You should have seen your face."

"Wow! He's sure tricky," Buster said pulling himself onto the dock.

They wrung out their shirts and laid them on the dock to dry as they watched the heron.

"Let's take turns. One of us can watch the heron; the other can watch that sly manatee," Buster suggested, settling back down on the dock.

Rob watched the heron; Buster watched the manatees.

After a while Rob gave up watching the heron and said, "We need to get on the other side of the *mangroves* so we can see him better."

"We could swim around the *mangroves* to the small spoil island to get a closer look," Buster suggested. "I've got some waxed bags from lunch to keep the scope dry."

Easing themselves back into the water with the wrapped scope held high, they swam for the island. Soon the baby manatee was right under them.

"Something rubbed against me," Rob said nervously.

"It's that sly manatee again, I bet," smiled Buster as the baby surfaced. "Now what's he trying to do?"

"Looks like he wants to know what's in the bag," Rob chuckled as they tread water.

Buster watched in amazement as the calf tried to taste the bag.

"He must like peanut butter and jelly, too. Hey! Let's call him Sly — Sly Manatee."

"That's a good name for him," Rob agreed.

The island was made from material left over from when the lock was constructed. Sometimes tools became exposed as the water washed the dirt and silt away. Buster found his old spotter's scope there the last time he went exploring.

Buster unwrapped the scope only to find that it was wet.

"Nuts! I'll have to dry it at home. We might as well look around," Buster grumbled.

As the boys explored, Sly and his three-year-old sister investigated the run-down dock by the lock. Its supports were almost rotted through, and the bank behind the dock was washed out, leaving a large pond full of hyacinths. A small opening between the dock's pilings was its only entrance. Sensing the danger, Sly's sister swam away. Sly reluctantly followed, eyeing the hyacinths. Leaving his sister, he swam back to see what the boys were doing.

"Wow! Look at this big crowbar," Rob called out.

"Tomorrow let's bring our floats and take it home," Buster suggested.

As they swam back to the dock, Sly occasionally rubbed against them.

"I guess he thinks we're one of them," Buster laughed. "He sure is a gentle guy."

When they got back to the dock, Sly watched as long as he could.

"Today was fun," Sly thought as he swam to his mother's side. "Hope they come again."

CHAPTER 3

~Not So Sly~

The next day, Buster and Rob returned to see if the heron was really Valiant. When they arrived, the heron was busy making final artistic judgments as to where his last stick should go in his nest. This is an important decision, because female herons choose mates with the most attractive nests.

"We will be able to get a good look at him today," Buster said looking at the nest.

"Hey, guess who's swimming toward us spinning spirals?" Rob quizzed.

"Let's swim like that!" they exclaimed at the same time.

Pulling off their shirts they dove into the water. It wasn't long before they mastered the manatee roll. It was follow the leader. Sly would roll, then the boys would roll. Sly would do a head-over-tail tumble, and the boys would follow holding their noses.

Suddenly, a loud cawing drew their attention back to the nest. A female heron had joined the male heron.

"NOW's the time! He's in full view," Rob said excitedly.

Buster swam ahead with the scope to the island. This time the scope was wrapped in a waterproof chart case. Reaching the shore, he unwrapped the scope and peered at the heron.

"It's Valiant! It's Valiant!" Buster cried out with joy as Rob came ashore.

"Let me see," Rob said reaching for the scope.

As the boys watched Valiant and his mate, Sly felt like having a hyacinth snack. He swam up to the dock by the lock and looked at the wall-to-wall hyacinths behind it. He found the gap he and his sister had seen before, and swam for the hyacinths. He was halfway through when he got stuck. He pushed and twisted and kicked with his tail.

Suddenly, he broke free, but behind him — Bang! — the dock collapsed.

He ate hyacinths in the shallow water until he was full, and then he thought of the boys. He swam to where he had come through, but the collapsed dock blocked his way.

"Let's see what Sly is up to," Buster suggested after Valiant and his mate flew off together.

They used the scope to look around; finally, they spotted his mother by the wrecked dock with Sly trapped.

"Sly's in trouble!" Buster yelled, dropping the scope on the island and running into the water. Rob was right behind him.

Reaching the area, they surveyed the situation.

"We need something to pry these boards free," Buster said.

"The crowbar! We need the crowbar we saw yesterday," Rob remembered.

Picking up the floats as they swam to the island, they dragged the bar to the water's edge and tied it to the floats.

Sly's mother was still at the collapsed dock with his sister.

"Don't worry," Buster said consolingly as he reached the area. "We'll get him out."

They studied the boards that blocked the way. One board was jammed between the two remaining supports for the dock. If they pried the board free, the dock would float downstream and clear the opening.

Grabbing the crowbar, they wedged it between the board and the support.

"One. Two. Three. Pull!" they hollered in unison at each other.

The wood gave way a little. They wedged the crowbar in deeper.

Again they shouted and tugged.

The wood gave way a little more.

Once more they shouted and tugged as hard as they could.

"Crack!"

Finally, the board gave way and the dock began to float away.

"You're clear Sly; come on out," Buster called.

Sly, however, decided to grab another snack or two and went back to enjoying the hyacinths. Realizing the tide was going out and that it would trap him again because it was getting too shallow, the boys acted quickly. Buster grabbed some of the hyacinths while Rob blocked Sly from eating any. Waving hyacinths in front of him, Buster kept backing out into deeper water. Sly kept following him until he was out of danger.

"Whew! We did it!" Buster sighed.

Sly happily nuzzled his mother as the boys swam back to the island to get the scope. The sun was almost setting and the boys knew they had to leave. Getting up on the dock they watched Sly roll and play with his sister.

"See you tomorrow, Sly," Buster said as they climbed the stairs.

On the way home, Buster reflected on the day he had just shared with his good friend Rob. He was thrilled to have found his old friend Valiant and to have met his new friend Sly. Realizing how unique his animal friends were, he looked forward to tomorrow.

The End

Glossary

Foraging: The act of searching for food. Manatees forage when they search for sea grasses they like to eat.

Lock: An enclosed part of a waterway equipped with a chamber that can raise or lower boats from one level to another.

Mangroves: Subtropical trees that grow in shallow water that have above-ground roots. These roots make an excellent habitat for baby fish to grow, giving them a place to hide from the bigger fish that try to eat them.

Sound: To dive suddenly downward through water.

Spill-way: A barrier built across a canal or stream that regulates the flow of water to help prevent flooding.

Warm Water Discharge: When the cooling water in a power plant gets warm, it is sent out to an area that mixes the warm water with cool lake water, creating a warm area. Manatees take advantage of these areas to keep warm in the colder days of winter.

More About Manatees

The name manatee is thought to come from the Carib word "manati." The Carib people lived on the Caribbean islands during the time of Columbus, but have since died out. West Indian manatees are among the gentlest of all sea creatures. They are semi-gregarious, with no hierarchy or natural enemies. A usual group consists of a mother and young. In winter, they gather in warm water sources like springs and discharges at power plants to keep warm. In groups, they nuzzle one another like hugging old friends. Sometimes, two and three-year-old manatees even baby-sit their younger brothers and sisters to give the mother a break. They seldom move fast, but are capable of quick movements when alarmed.

Manatees can weigh more than 3,000 pounds and be 13 feet long; however, most average 10 feet long and weigh 1,000 pounds. It's possible they can live up to 60 years. Gestation lasts 13 months, with the birth of usually one calf, three to four feet long, weighing 60 to 70 pounds. The young stay with their mother for up to five years, learning the migration and habits necessary for survival. Their round bodies vary in color from gray to brown, and taper to a paddle-like tail. When swimming, a manatee uses its tail for propulsion and steers with its front flippers.

Manatees' eyes are small and beady. In clear water they are able to see objects, in color, 30 feet or more away. They communicate with chirps, whistles, clicks and perhaps, infrasound (sounds too low for the human ear to hear). Mother and calf have been able to find each other even in the most turbid or cloudy water. This suggests both communication and sound location.

Manatees are the only marine mammal that eats vegetation exclusively. Being vegetarians, manatees must eat large quantities of seagrass, hyacinths and other vegetation. They eat up to 15% of their body weight every day to maintain their strength, and spend most of their time grazing in shallow water.

A natural condition inherent in manatees is very detrimental to them. They cannot hear the sound frequency of boats well enough to know where a boat is coming from, or how close it is. Many boat owners disregard warnings posted in areas inhabited by manatees. This is very dangerous for them, and causes up to 25% of yearly manatee casualties.

In addition to the boats, habitat destruction is making life more difficult for manatees. Seagrass beds in many areas where manatees used to graze have been destroyed by dredging and smothered by silt from drainage. The lack of seagrass in these areas has made it necessary for manatees to change their eating habits and even their migration paths for food. They range throughout the southeast coast of the United States and parts of northern South America.

"Beauty is in the eye of the beholder" is an old cliché that fits the manatee. Its pug nose reminds some people of dogs that are so homely they're cute. Their elephant-like skin is rough, with hairs sparsely scattered over its body to help detect touch or movement. When a manatee swims, the grace and beauty of its movements reminds one of a beautiful ballet. Perhaps that is why scientists gave them the name derived from Greek mythology, "Sirenia," and ancient sailors mistook them for mermaids.

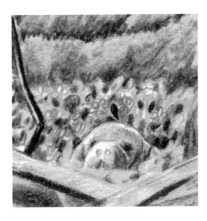

Manatee Boating Safety

Manatees Were Placed on the Endangered Species List in 1973

When boating in manatee areas PLEASE:

• Wear polarized sunglasses. They eliminate the glare of the sun and help boaters to see below the water's surface.

• Stay in deep water channels. Avoid boating over seagrass beds and shallow areas where manatees might be feeding. Be aware that manatees also use deep water channels.

• Look for a snout, back, tail or flipper breaking the surface of the water, or a flat spot on the water that is created by the motion of the manatee's paddle-shaped tail when it dives or swims.

• If you see a manatee when operating a powerboat, remain at a safe distance. Fifty feet is suggested. If you want to observe the manatee, cut the motor, but do not drift over the animal.

• If you like to jet-ski, water-ski, or participate in high-speed water sports, choose areas manatees do not, or cannot frequent, such as a land-locked lake.

• Obey posted speed zone signs and keep away from posted manatee sanctuaries.

About the Author

John Harms II was born in Dearborn, Michigan, and grew up in Palm Beach County, Florida. Many of his stories originate from his experiences as a young boy. During his youth, he spent time in the local forests and enjoyed the animals. Manatees and sea grasses were plentiful in the waterways by his home, and deserted coconut plantations gave him a colorful backdrop for his stories.

Mr. Harms II graduated from University College at the University of Florida in 1971. He went on to design and patent filtration equipment to purify water and other liquids, while compiling his adventures. His stories educate and encourage people, especially children, to care about their environment. He visits schools often, giving presentations about writing, publishing and ecology.

His life is shared with his wife, three children, two dogs, one cat, a bird and countless fish.

Also Read Buster's Other Adventures:

Book One

The Saving of Arma Armadillo

ISBN 0-9653871-1-9

Book Two

The Saving Of Valiant Blue Heron

ISBN 0-9653871-7-8

Available through bookstores and from Frederick Press

Look for these upcoming titles by John Harms II from Frederick Press:

Manatee Freedom

and

The Mystery of No-Name Island

Frederick Press
P. O. Box 32593
Palm Beach Gardens,
Florida 33420
(561) 625-4964